Anneena was on the beach with W...
and Wilma. It was sunny, but the sea
was chilly.

There were lots of people on the beach.
Wilf had a frisbee.
"Catch," he called.

Anneena ran to catch the frisbee.
She nearly ran into some children.
The children looked upset.

The children were lost.
"We can't see Mummy and Daddy,"
said the girl.

The children were called Lily and Charlie. Anneena and Wilma took them to the Lost Children's Hut.

"We will wait with you until your mummy comes," said Anneena.

"Let me tell you a story," said Anneena.
"In a far off land, there was a princess.
But she had a problem ..."

The princess was called Sophie.
The problem was her sneezing.

When she sneezed, it sounded as if she was saying funny things, like 'cheesy feet' or 'stinky socks'.

People said Sophie was shouting at them. They did not like it.

The queen was cross with Sophie.
"You need better manners," she said.

"Mossy teeth!" Sophie sneezed into her handkerchief.

Even the king was cross with Sophie.
"Tut, tut," he said. "You bad girl."
Sophie sneezed harder and harder.

"I do not mean to be bad," said Sophie. "But when I am sneezing, people think I am shouting at them."

Sophie was so unhappy that she ran
off.  She ran deep into the forest.
But soon she was lost.

She sat down on a bed of leaves.
"I will rest my head on these leaves,"
she said, and she soon fell fast asleep.

She was asleep all night. To her relief,
there were no sneezes at all.

Sophie sat up with a start. A field mouse, an owl and a donkey were looking at her.

"You must be the sneezing princess," said the little mouse.

"Yes, I am," said Sophie. "But out here in the forest I have not sneezed at all."

"People are always sneezing," said the donkey. "There is too much dust in their houses."

The king and queen ran up. "Sophie!" said the king. "We have found you. What a relief!"

Just then, Charlie saw his mummy. "Charlie! Lily!" she said. "I have found you! What a relief!"

"We did like the story," said Lily.
"Did Sophie stop sneezing?"
"What do you think?" asked Anneena.

Yes, if they did the dusting!